This edition published by Parragon Books Ltd in 2015
and distributed by

Parragon Inc.
440 Park Avenue South, 13th Floor
New York, NY 10016
www.parragon.com

ISBN 978-1-4723-9635-8

Printed in China

Bath · New York · Cologne · Melbourne · Delhi
Hong Kong · Shenzhen · Singapore · Amsterdam

Mickey woke up and jumped out of bed.
As he slipped his feet into his slippers,
Mickey said "Good morning" to Pluto,
just like he did every day.

Mickey ate his breakfast, like he did every day.
He brushed his teeth, like he did every day.
And he did his stretches, like he did every day.
But today was not like every other day.

Today was Mickey's birthday!

"What should we do today?" Mickey asked Pluto.
But Pluto wasn't paying attention to Mickey.
He was staring out of the window.

Mickey looked out of the window, too.
His friends were walking past his house.
"I wonder what they're doing,"
Mickey said to himself.

Mickey looked more closely. Donald was carrying cups and plates. Daisy was carrying lemonade. Goofy was carrying a bunch of balloons. And Minnie was carrying a big cake.

"Pluto!" Mickey shouted. "It looks like they're having a party!" Mickey looked out of the window again. "Do you think they know it's my birthday? Could they be having a birthday party ... for me?"

"We'd better get dressed, Pluto," Mickey said. "Just in case!"

So Mickey dusted off his gloves and polished his buttons. He even brushed Pluto.

Soon, they were ready.

Mickey and Pluto sat in the living room, waiting for their friends. They waited ... and waited. But no one came.

Finally, the doorbell rang. Mickey jumped up and raced to the door. He threw it open, ready for his party. But there was no party outside. There was only Donald, and he looked upset. "What's wrong, Donald?" Mickey asked.

"My favorite hammock is broken,"
Donald told Mickey. "What am I going to do?
I can't nap without it! Can you help me fix it?"
Mickey knew his friend needed his help.
  "Sure, Donald," he said. "Let's go!"

So Donald, Mickey, and Pluto set off to fix the hammock. As they walked, an idea popped into Mickey's head.

Maybe there is no broken hammock, he thought. *Maybe Donald is really taking me to my party!*

Mickey was so excited that he started to skip.

Donald led Mickey to his garden.
He stopped in front of two trees and
looked down. There, on the ground,
was the broken hammock.

Mickey looked around. There were no balloons and no cake. There was just one friend who needed his help. So Mickey helped Donald fix his hammock.

"That should do it," Mickey said as he finished tying the hammock's rope around a tree.

"Thanks, Mickey!" Donald said when the hammock was strung up between the trees again.

Donald climbed into his hammock and was soon drifting off to sleep.

"You're welcome," Mickey said, and he started to head home.

"I guess there wasn't a party after all," Mickey said Just then, he heard Minnie and Daisy calling him. They wanted to show him something!

So Mickey went with Minnie and Daisy. As he walked, Mickey began to wonder about a party again.

Maybe they are taking me to my party! he thought.

Minnie and Daisy led Mickey to their flower garden.

"Ta-da!" said Daisy.

"Everything is blooming!" said Minnie.

Mickey looked around. The garden was full of flowers. And they were pretty. Still, Mickey couldn't help but be disappointed.

"Do you want to help us garden?" Minnie asked.

Mickey thought about it. He didn't have any other plans, so he helped water the flowers.

A few minutes later, Goofy ran up.

"Mickey! Mickey!" he shouted, tugging on his
friend's arm. "You've got to see this. I've never
seen anything like it!"

Mickey waved goodbye to Minnie and Daisy
as he rushed away with Goofy.

Goofy seems very excited, Mickey thought as his friend rushed him down the road. *I wonder what he wants to show me.*

Then Mickey realized, Goofy must be taking him to his party!

Suddenly, Goofy stopped running.
"Look, Mickey," he said, pointing to a large rock.
Mickey looked all around, but there was no sign
of a party. Why was Goofy so excited?

Then Mickey looked down. Two snails were
racing on the rock.

"Gosh! Watch 'em go!" Goofy said. "Have you
ever seen anything so exciting?"

Mickey had never seen a snail race before.
It was exciting, but not as exciting as a party!

Mickey and Pluto watched the snails race for a while. Then they headed home.

"Oh, well, Pluto," Mickey said. "I guess I was wrong. I guess there won't be a party after all."

Pluto whimpered. He had never seen Mickey look so sad.

Mickey hung his head low. How could everyone have
forgotten his birthday?

Mickey walked up the path to his house. He opened
the front door and stepped inside.

He reached for the light switch and....

"Surprise!"

Mickey's friends jumped out at him. They *had* planned a party after all. A surprise party! For the first time all day, Mickey had not expected it.

"I don't understand," he said. "I thought you were all busy today. How did you find time to plan a party … at my house … without me finding out?"

Minnie giggled. "We took turns keeping you busy," she explained.

Mickey smiled a huge smile. He was glad his friends
had tricked him. He loved surprise parties!

"Thanks, everyone," Mickey said, "for the best party
ever! And the best birthday!"

Mickey's friends clapped, whooped, and cheered,
"Happy birthday, Mickey!"